MW00907391

Thank God for your G.A.!

Arlene Hebert

3-8-2020

Endorsements

"The Angels are out of training and on the job! Arlene Hebert's delightful duo, Anjo and Angelle, are stationed inside an expectant mom, alongside her twins while they develop and grow.

Join them on a one-of-a-kind trip to inner space and learn how they all fit in such tight quarters, and why they have to wear stylish swimwear and goggles.

Peter DeHart's stunning graphics propel the reader through the creation of life as the twins and their guardian angels bump, kick and nudge their way to an important birthday—forty weeks away."

- **Frank Remkiewicz**
Children's Book Author & Illustrator

"Children are naturally curious beings. Oftentimes, however, they don't have enough information to formulate a question. In this fourth book of the Angeltale Adventure Series, Arlene Hebert provides children with the kind of help parents will appreciate. She takes a subject many adults are reluctant to discuss and places it in plain sight, in simple words and visual imagery children will understand. This is in addition to establishing a lifetime awareness of the beginning of life, not at birth, but at conception. Not only does she do all that, she does it well. The incomparable illustrations by artist Peter Berchman DeHart add to children's imagination, and the Let's Talk About section will provide exciting and personally eyeopening times for children."

- **Shirley Comeaux, Ph.D.**
Educator and Reading Specialist

"As a parent and pro-life advocate, I am thankful to have a book like this available for our children. This book helps children understand the perfection of the growing baby and why it is our duty to protect them. Not only did my daughter enjoy the story, but mom did, too!"

- Abby Johnson
Advocate for Life, Author of "unPLANNED"

"Arlene Hebert" weaves a fascinating story about the unique beauty of God's creation, making it both interesting and thought provoking for all ages!"

- James B. Godchaux, M.D. & Mrs. Kathleen D. Godchaux

"The fourth episode of the angels' adventures on Earth is a wonderful and fascinating story describing the development and growth of two fetuses in the mother's womb. The author and the illustrator have succeeded in depicting the physical environment of the womb, along with the developmental stages of the twins, in a very simplistic and precise manner."

- F.M. Hindelang, Jr., M.D.

"A true gift to the world, this book is a perfect combination of the extraordinary process of human creation and celebration of life. The pages are rich in description, expressed with delicate details of the beautiful uniqueness of each human life. This miraculous journey of childbirth is simply enlightening, revealing itself for the youngest reader to understand, wise enough to inspire the oldest of souls and can speak to the hearts of all ages. This book also teaches the importance of God as our creator, while instilling spiritual guidance, faith, life lessons for all ages to appreciate. A reminder to us all, that we are on a path of purpose and perfection through God's wisdom and plan."

- M. Maitland Deland, M.D.
Children's Book Author

"As a physician who delivers babies, I found Arlene Hebert's book to be informative and accurate on the aspects of fetal development, yet easy to understand for both adult and child alike. Her creative addition of angeology to the development process should stir the reader to both imagination and an appreciation for God's creative work. The book should foster an appreciation for the gift of life."

- Kim Hardey, M.D.

"The fourth book is a beautiful description of the miracle of life at the moment of conception that captures God's precious children as he brings them into the world. Angelle and Anjo ride a wave of adventure in a pool of amniotic fluid that has them swimming daily, watching in awe as Sarah and Matthew develop before their eyes! Children will love reading this wonderful story that illustrates Father God's unimaginable love for all of us! What a blessing to be able to read this to my children at bedtime; thank you Arlene for sharing your wonderful gift to all!"

- Jude Bares, M.D

This Book Belongs to . . .

. . . .

name

Thank you for purchasing book four of the Angeltale Adventure Series. This book represents a miracle to me personally. You see, writing for children was never a dream of mine. This was all God's idea.

This book was fun to write since I was able to use my professional background as a registered nurse. Although it's fiction, real fetal growth and development facts are woven into the story.

I believe that the creation of life comes from God. I compare witnessing the birth of babies to witnessing real miracles that life offers.

I promise this story will make many giggle as they recall their own personal experiences dealing with the births of their loved ones.

Enjoy the story and God Bless!

Arlene Hebert

To Purchase Books and Products

Visit the new and exciting website for children, **www.angeltaleadventures.com**, where copies of all books and release dates of upcoming Angeltale Adventures are available in the Angeltale Book Store.

Limited Edition prints of the artwork featured throughout this book and others are available for purchase in the Book Store as well. All prints are available in black and white with selected prints in color. These frame-ready prints, signed and numbered by the artist, can be hung in classrooms, children's rooms or collected by children of all ages.

Become a member of Angeltale Adventures on **Facebook** to keep up with the development of products and future books.

The Angel Brigade Club

If we as adults believe that the future of the world belongs to the children of today, then we MUST help teach children NOW how to make better choices.

The Angel Brigade Club was created for that purpose. The club will help unite children and encourage them to make better choices in their lives. Through one good decision at a time, children can change the future of the world.

This club teaches children that angels are real; they are all around us. As Christians, we believe that there is that special angel entrusted to assist and guide each one of us through life. These invisible servants of God are standing ready to help; we just have to call on them. ANGEL POWER ACTIVATE!

Visit **www.angeltaleadventures.com** to enroll in the club. Children are encouraged to name their guardian angels, sign the Book of Life (featured in book two of the series), take the pledge – Take Back Our World – and print the frame-ready certificate, print the FREE quarterly newsletters and purchase the club T-shirt. The Angel Brigade Club Quarterly Newsletter NO. 1 has ideas for newly-forming clubs. Unique club ideas can be shared by e-mailing me through the site. Your idea could be featured in future newsletters.

Please help me make this a wonderful opportunity for our children and grandchildren.

G.A.'s on Assignment

G.A.'s on Assignment

Written by
Arlene B. Hebert

Illustrated by
Peter Berchman DeHart

Book Four

Angeltale Adventures

Miss Doll Publishing
A Division of Miss Doll, Inc.
Lafayette, Louisiana

Angeltale Adventures

The Angeltale Adventures and all book titles, characters and locales original to The Angeltale Adventure Series are trademarks of Arlene Hebert. Use without permission is strictly prohibited.

G.A.'s on Assignment
First Edition Copyright © 2011 Arlene Hebert
All Illustrations © 2011 Peter Berchman DeHart

Library of Congress Cataloging in Publication Data
ISBN 13: 9780981926438

Published by Miss Doll Publishing
A Division of Miss Doll, Inc.
P. O. Box 63034
Lafayette, Louisiana 70596-3034

Illustrated by Peter DeHart
Design and layout by Peter DeHart of Makemade, LLC
Edited by Shirley Comeaux, Ph.D., Nancy Burns, Joyce Michel, Michelle Truxillo and Sonja Davis
Printed in the United States of America

Dedication

To Almighty God, my loving Father in Heaven;
I love you, Father, with all that I am;
Thank You for loving me.
This book is my little gift to You.
I promise always to be a "pencil in Your Hand."

Contents

ADVENTURES ON EARTH BEGIN

Angelle and Anjo marched down the aisle of the great hall followed by other student angels. They stood tall and proud as the newest guardian angels in Heaven. Anjo broke silence.

"I can't believe we made it," Anjo whispered to Angelle.

"Sh-hh-hh," Angelle placed her finger across her mouth. "No talking, remember?" she mouthed.

At last graduation day arrived. The G.A.S.,
Guardian Angel School, seemed to last an eternity
for all of them. Graduating as full-fledged guardian
angels was the wish of all little angels, especially
Angelle and Anjo. They stood out among all the
angels because they were God's chosen team for
the special twins assignment. Angelle and Anjo
were dressed in the finest angel robes designed
especially for them. Extra-polished halos and
the fluffiest pairs of special-made wings
complemented their garments.

All the student angels bowed and knelt
down before God. God said a few words to the
audience of angels about how proud He was of all
the students. He gave them the special guardian
angel blessing and said:

"I bless thee with the graces

That will help all of you

Protect My children on Earth.

You are now part of

My Holy Army."

They were so excited when God presented each diploma with the word "Passed" stamped in gold.

The moment every angel in Heaven had been waiting for had finally arrived. God was ready to create the twins, Sarah and Matthew. Angelle and Anjo were called forth and stood before God.

"My precious world must change," God said. "Angelle, Anjo, I'm counting on you two to teach Sarah and Matthew the proper ways to live. They will teach My other children mostly by their actions and their words. The souls of all My children on Earth are important to Me," He stressed. The love that radiated from God took the angels' breath away.

"Do you have any last-minute questions?" God asked.

"No, Father, we are ready," Angelle answered for both of them.

"When you arrive on Earth, I have a surprise for each of you," God said.

The word surprise brought a big smile to their faces. Angelle and Anjo turned toward each other as God raised His arms upward. They held hands when a strong wind tousled their hair about, and their wings flapped naturally in the inviting currents. They rose above the crowd of angels and began to spin creating a heavenly tornado. Lightning bolts escaped when clouds and stars were pulled into their whirlwind of energy. They pointed toward Earth and waited.

God lowered His arms downward as electrifying rays shot forth from the palms of His hands. At that moment, God created Sarah and Matthew in their mother's womb. The adventure begins like this...

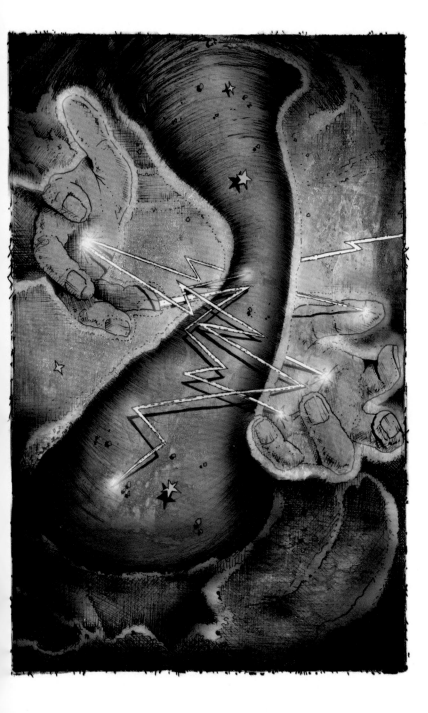

LIFE BEGINS ON EARTH

Faster than the blink of an eye, Angelle and Anjo were transported to Earth. They didn't know what to expect, since they had never been on Earth before. One thing for sure, they were now G.A.'s — guardian angels — on assignment. They didn't have time to think about their surprises.

"It's pretty dark in here," Anjo whispered.

"I know," Angelle said. "Let's turn up our

halos so we can see."

As their halo lights beamed brightly, they could see their new home. What a different place this was. It was small, warm and quiet. This would be their home for the next forty weeks.

"Is it my imagination, or are we real small?" Anjo asked.

"We're inside the mother," Angelle reminded him. "We are small, and we'll get smaller as the human cells grow into babies."

"Look at all the ripples in the walls. And look at those things." Anjo pointed to large and small tubes that connected everywhere.

"They must be arteries and veins; they carry the mother's blood," Angelle said, always knowing the right answers.

"Cool!" Anjo said. "Anatomy of the human body is so interesting."

Angelle glanced at Anjo and began to giggle. She realized what Anjo's surprise was. "Where did Father come up with those swimming trunks?"

Anjo stopped checking out their new home and looked at Angelle. "Are you laughing at me?" Anjo asked focusing his eyes on Angelle. He too began to chuckle.

"Why are YOU laughing at me," she asked.

"Look at your outfit. It's pretty snazzy," Anjo said.

Angelle glanced downward expecting to see her beautiful angel garment designed for graduation. It was replaced by some sort of apparel that stopped above her knees. "Oh my word," she shrieked trying to pull the hem down to her ankles. "It's so short!"

Anjo was laughing so much that he rolled into the water. He climbed out of the watery stuff and put his arm around Angelle who was now chuckling with him.

"You have to admit, Father does have the greatest sense of humor," Anjo said. "These are the best surprises. We must remember to teach Matthew and Sarah to laugh."

They soon recovered from their laughing fits and continued exploring their new home. Anjo's face immediately turned from excitement and fun — to panic. His gaze traveled from one area of their tiny home to another. "Where are they? I can't find Matthew and Sarah."

"Calm down. They're right over there," she said and pointed.

Anjo spotted two tiny clumps of cells floating in a little tunnel. He breathed a sigh of relief. One clump was bigger than the other. He flew to the larger clump of cells and placed his hand over it. "This must be Matthew. I can't wait to see him grow from this little clump to a big, strong, baby boy."

Angelle and Anjo together examined the two little clumps of cells when suddenly their halos beamed brightly. This was their signal from God that He had something special to tell them. They immediately grew quiet.

"This is the beginning of life on Earth," God communicated to them. As they understood His message, they were in awe at the little clumps of cells. These cells would one day become little persons who would run and play with them.

"Amazing," Angelle said. "We're real guardian angels now."

"Yes. We're their protectors till the day they return to Heaven. That makes me feel proud," Anjo said.

Angelle nodded. "Me, too."

ANGELLE AND ANJO
LIVE IN TIGHT QUARTERS

One week passed. The clumps of cells moved down the tunnel into the larger room. They attached to the walls of this room where they continued to grow. As they grew, fluid surrounded and protected them.

Angelle and Anjo had fun in this room. Swimming became a daily exercise.

"What's this place called again?" he asked.

"Uterus," she answered.

"Earth has so many funny words. We have a lot to remember." Anjo swam from one side to the other. "Being a guardian angel is easy so far."

"It's easy now, but once the twins are born, we'll never be bored," Angelle said.

Anjo agreed. "It's cozy in here. I could live here forever."

"Don't forget. We'll get smaller as the babies

grow larger. It won't always be cozy in here. Living in these tight quarters will seem like a long time."

"Hum-m-m, I never thought about that," he said. "I won't be able to swim any more. Oh well! We told Father we were going to be the best guardian angels He ever made. That's our mission and our promise."

Angelle jumped high into the watery stuff and joined Anjo. "And we will be the best that we can be!"

ANGELLE AND ANJO DANCE TO THE RHYTHM OF THE BEATS

Angelle and Anjo kept watchful eyes day and night as the tiny clumps of cells grew bigger. Sarah's and Matthew's heads and the rest of their bodies began to take shape. Twenty-two days went by.

Angelle and Anjo rested on their favorite spots. Suddenly they heard a strange noise. It sounded like someone beating on a drum.

Ba-bum, ba-bum, ba-bum.

They sat up quickly. "What's that?" Angelle
asked.

As their eyes searched every inch of their

living quarters, Anjo spotted Matthew's heart moving. "It's beating; it's really beating!"

They hovered over Matthew's tiny body. It was only one inch long. They saw his heart working with their special angelic vision. They watched in awe and became excited with each beat. "One, two, three, four, five, six," they counted together.

"Being angels is the best!" Anjo said. "I like seeing these special things."

"I can't believe his tiny heart is beating in only twenty-two days. I wish Sarah's heart would hurry up and beat."

No sooner did Angelle utter her words, Sarah's heart began beating. "Two hearts beating!" she shouted. "Let's celebrate!"

Together Angelle and Anjo danced to the rhythm of the beats, singing:

God is Love and Love is God.

The miracle of God is life.

The miracle of life is God!

When they calmed down, they examined the rest of the little bodies, especially the brains. After looking at each brain, Anjo said, "I can tell already that Matthew will be known as Matthew Genius. Just look at the size of his brain."

"Right! And what about my Sarah's brain? Since they're twins, she's going to be smart, too. I'll call her Sarah Genius."

"OK; they'll both be smart geniuses." Anjo continued, "One day Matthew will grow up to be a president, 'cause he'll be so smart."

Angelle interrupted again, placing her hands on her hips, "You keep forgetting my Sarah!"

"I'm only kidding. They'll both be presidents together and solve the problems of the world. Now come and dance with me to the rhythm of the beats!"

Angelle and Anjo looked forward to each new day with excitement. Miracles took place continuously as the itty-bitty clumps of cells changed before their eyes. The uterus became known to them as the place where miracles happened daily. Although they would live in this temporary home for a short period of time, Angelle and Anjo would remember it forever.

IT'S A DOUBLE SURPRISE

Up and down, up and down, Angelle and Anjo bounced. Around and around they were thrown. Noises echoed loudly outside the uterus.

"Is there a storm out there?" Anjo asked, as he was thrown around in the watery stuff.

Angelle held on tightly. Pulling herself closely to the wall of the uterus, she put her ears to it. "Shush!" she said listening to the sounds outside.

"Three people are talking," Angelle said. "A

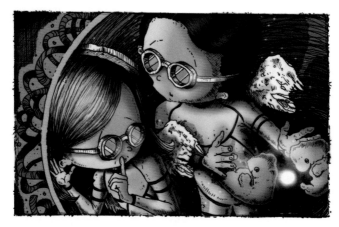

man is telling someone that he loves...," then it dawned on her. "Sarah and Matthew's mother and father just found out from the doctor that they're expecting," Angelle said. "Yes, she's pregnant!" Angelle shouted.

Anjo shook his head. "Wait a minute! You're telling me that their parents didn't know we're all in here!" he said in disbelief. "We've been right here for six weeks protecting Matthew and Sarah, and they had no idea that we're on duty!"

"I know you're upset, but people don't know everything like we do. We're angels! That's just the way it is on Earth."

"I know," he said disappointed. "It's just that I want everyone to know we're in here."

"They will, in time." She placed her arm around Anjo's shoulder.

Anjo was thoughtful. "I remember when Father told us about Matthew and Sarah, long before He created them in here. He even named them," he said.

"And I remember Father telling us about Sarah and Matthew's mom and dad, how they would be high school sweethearts and marry six years later," Angelle added and sighed. "Father God is so romantic!"

"Here you go again. You get that goofy look on your face when you talk about love," Anjo said.

"I know. I can't wait for Sarah to fall in love."

"Fall in love! Sarah hasn't been born yet, and you're getting her married. Snap out of it. We have thirty-four more weeks left to live in here," Anjo said and laughed. "Now come swim with me; the watery fluid is warm. It might do your angel-brain some good."

Angelle and Anjo continued to celebrate the good news. They knew the world would soon know that not one baby, but two babies were growing in the small quarters—a double surprise. Surprise! Surprise!

GOD'S PLAN
IS AN AWESOME PLAN

God and all the angels in Heaven enjoyed watching Angelle and Anjo as the babies developed. Angelle and Anjo took their jobs seriously.

"Angelle, I'm a little concerned!"

"Why? The babies are growing well."

"I guess," his voice sounded unsure.

"OK, what's the matter?" she asked.

23

"Look, Sarah has ten fingers and ten toes. My Matthew has ten fingers and eight toes. How is he going to run and play ball with only eight toes?"

"That's what you're worried about," she said. "We've only been in here eleven weeks. Just give Matthew a few more days. Those two toes will finish growing, and his feet will be perfect. I promise!"

Her words soothed Anjo.   "Thanks,

Angelle; you're the best angel-buddy. I'm glad we're together."

"Anjo, look how cute our assignments are. They're almost twelve weeks old. Their little bodies are nearly all formed; their brains are working; their hearts are beating. They've been swimming around in here since they were seven weeks old. How much do you think they weigh?"

"Hum-m-m!" He shifted backward examining the size of each and stroked his chin. "Each one is about three inches long. I'd say they'd each weigh about twenty jelly beans worth," Anjo said as he chuckled.

"That makes sense to me. We do need to think in earthly ways, since we're on Earth. And jelly beans are real sweet, just like Sarah and Matthew," Angelle said giggling.

"It's really amazing how Father came up with this plan — babies growing inside their mothers. What an awesome plan!" Anjo said.

"A really awesome plan!" Angelle agreed.

ANJO RAPS
TO HIS CREATION

Anjo often took inventory of the little bodies while they grew. He was greatly relieved when Matthew's last toe appeared.

Angelle and Anjo were amazed as they watched clumps of cells develop into two tiny, little persons. They learned in their studies that the first three months (twelve weeks) were the most important.

During this period of time, Sarah's and Matthew's organs—the brain, the heart, the lungs, the kidneys—everything developed completely. All the tiny organs were working. After twelve weeks, the little bodies only grew larger.

"I can't wait for them to talk to us. I'm going to teach Matthew to sing," Anjo said.

"Sing? What's with singing? You can't sing!"

"I sure can."

"Show me," she challenged.

Anjo settled himself on a nice flat surface while Angelle took a seat.

"OK, here goes my own creation." He straightened his halo, fluffed his wings, cleared his throat and bowed. "The name of my musical composition is," he thought for a moment, then smiled, "Angel Rap." He began.

"Brothers and sisters, on the Earth below,

You can do the dance that the angels know.

Just stand up straight, hold your head high,

Relax those shoulders, you're about to fly.

Dance to the music that the Lord has made,

This is going to be a wild parade.

Oh, ah-ah, oh-oh-oh-oh, ah!

Oh, ah-ah, oh-oh-oh-oh, ah!"

Anjo's spirit body moved to a be-bop rhythm, and Angelle rolled in laughter.

"You're not only an angel, you're a funny and entertaining angel!" she said.

Anjo ignored her and rapped on.

"Now angels, angels, fall in line,

Snugly tuck your wings behind.

Turn in a circle at your very place,

That will release God's saving grace.

Now spin those halos shined nicely and bright,

To move about the Earth on the darkest night;

To guard your charges, so they won't fall,

Into Satan's hand, that's the worst of all!

Oh, ah-ah, oh-oh-oh-oh, ah!

Oh, ah-ah, oh-oh-oh-oh, ah!"

Angelle joined Anjo as he jammed to

his song. Their dancing stirred up bubbles and disturbed Sarah and Matthew. Small kicks from the babies hit the walls of their temporary home, the uterus.

Sarah and Matthew's mother felt the movement. She put both of her hands on her abdomen. It felt like she had butter-flies inside her tummy. She wondered if she was feeling the life of her babies for the first time. She smiled to herself.

Meanwhile inside, Angelle and Anjo, not aware of the commotion they were causing, kept on jamming. Anjo continued and made up the verses as he went.

"Now, children, children, listen to me,

This is no foolishness, I guarantee.

Dancing to the music of the Heavenly King,

Is serious business, not a wild thing!

You're important creatures of the Lord above,

Made from His infinite wisdom and love.

Molded and shaped into beings of His,

By His precious hands, in His likeness you live!

Oh, ah-ah, oh-oh-oh-oh, ah!

Oh, ah-ah, oh-oh-oh-oh, ah!

So all together now!

Swing those hips and move those feet,

Jump in all directions and take the great leap;

Listen to the music and feel that beat,

The music of the Lord is always-s-s so sweet!

Oh, ah-ah, oh-oh-oh-oh, ah!

Oh, ah-ah, oh-oh-oh-oh, ah!"

THE BABIES ARE DISTURBED

By the time Anjo finished with his rap song, the babies were greatly disturbed. Kicks were flying.

"Who taught them karate?" Anjo asked as he darted away from little feet.

"It may look like karate, and it may feel like karate, but it's not. You need to stop your rapping." Angelle, too, was busy protecting herself. "It's dangerous in here when both of the babies are this active."

Suddenly the babies forced their eyes open and uttered little sounds. They blinked several times, then fixed their eyes on Angelle and Anjo. For the first time, Sarah and Matthew saw their guardian angels. It was a treasured moment for all of them.

Anjo stood tall and began, "I'm your guardian angel. I'm Anjo, and you're Matthew."

Angelle looked into Sarah's big brown eyes and introduced herself, too. "I'm Angelle, and you're Sarah." Sarah blinked as if she understood.

"Hiccup, hiccup," came out of Matthew's little mouth.

"Now, what's the matter? Did you swallow too much fluid during your karate performance?" Anjo asked Matthew.

"Oh, Anjo, babies get the hiccups," Angelle said. "Don't you remember studying that, or did you skip that lesson, too?"

Again there was a burst of movement between the babies. Matthew moved his hand toward Anjo and accidentally hooked Anjo's wing. Matthew then moved his hand toward his mouth.

"Help, Angelle," Anjo hollered, "he's trying to eat me."

Angelle laughed and flew towards Anjo to set him free.

"What's so funny?" Anjo asked. "Matthew was trying to eat me! Wasn't he?"

"Oh! Anjo, you do have a lot to learn. Babies like to suck their thumbs." The two angels looked on as Matthew settled down once again with his thumb in his mouth.

Anjo listened to the sucking sounds Matthew was making. "You're right," Anjo said as he laughed at himself. "I do have a lot to learn."

THE BIG EXIT DAY ARRIVES

After the first twelve weeks, Angelle and Anjo continued to shrink in size while Sarah and Matthew grew larger. Their swimming trunks also adjusted to their smaller sizes—special angelic technology developed for this assignment. The four of them lived together the best way they could.

Papa God was very pleased as He and the angels watched from above. Things happened with Sarah and Matthew just the way God planned them to. Every body part of the babies grew at just the right time. Sarah and Matthew lived in their mother's uterus for forty weeks.

Then one night while Sarah and Matthew were sound asleep, and Angelle and Anjo were resting comfortably, things began to happen. The four of them were tossed around inside the mother. Anjo ended up with a big toe in his ear.

"What's the matter out there? Can't the mother stay still so the babies can sleep in here," Anjo complained.

"Anjo, it's time!"

"Time for what?"

"Time for our assignments to meet their parents and the world," Angelle shouted excitedly. "It may be a little rough trip into the world, but the babies are ready to be born."

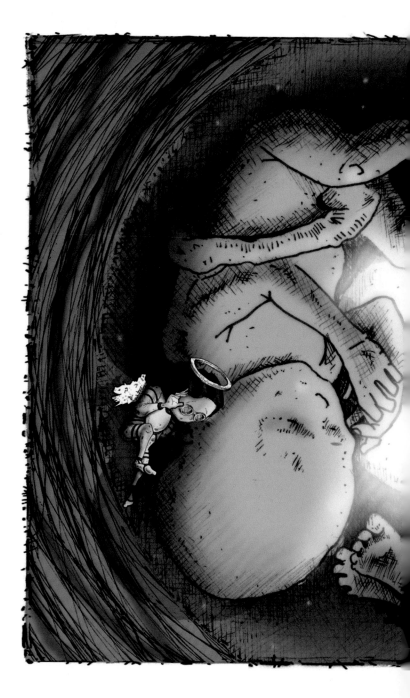

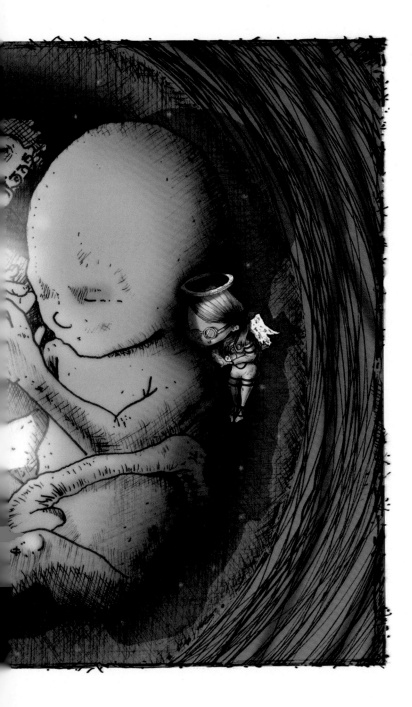

Anjo became nervous. "What can I do? Where should I wait? Should I push Matthew out? Do I go out first? Maybe I should catch him?"

"Take a deep breath! Calm down, you're acting like their father," Angelle said.

"Yeah, you're right. I have to calm down; I'm only an angel. One, two, three, four," he counted while breathing deep and slow. "OK, now what should I do?"

When Anjo saw how calm and collected Angelle was, he was embarrassed. "Well, I'm just excited," he said, trying to excuse his behavior. "Matthew will never have a baby, so I went over that angel lesson only one time. I guess all I have to do is stick with Matthew and Papa God will do the rest."

"You got it!" Angelle said.

The ride to the hospital was quick and bumpy. When they arrived, the mother was placed in a wheelchair and taken quickly to the delivery room.

Matthew was the first to be born. He came out screaming, and Anjo followed him. The lights were so bright that it took a while for Anjo's eyes to adjust. When he saw what one of the nurses was doing to poor little Matthew, Anjo called out to her, "Oh my word! Cover his little body. He has angel-bumps all over." But the nurse couldn't hear him. "He's going to catch a cold," he shouted.

Sarah was born three minutes after Matthew, and Angelle was by her side. "Come on Sarah, let them hear your sweet voice; sing for me," Angelle said. At first a tiny whimper could be heard; then a loud melody of crying began.

"Wow, she's got a nice pair of lungs!" Angelle said surprised.

Angelle and Anjo observed doctors, nurses and their guardian angels moving about the delivery room, caring for Sarah and Matthew. Angelle had to reassure Anjo that everything was going according to God's plan and would be fine.

The birth of their assignments was an awesome event. In a trance, Anjo asked, "What did Papa God call this again?"

Angelle answered, also in a daze, "He called this the Miracle of Life."

"It sure is!" Anjo said. "It sur-r-re is!"

THE SECOND CELEBRATION TAKES PLACE

And so it was on this day, Sarah and Matthew blessed the world with their presence. They were finally born after forty weeks of living in tight quarters.

Heaven celebrated their earthly birthdays with another celebration. The first celebration was on Creation Day, the day when God created them in their mother's womb. Their names were recorded in the Big Book in Heaven with Angelle's and Anjo's names next to them.

Sarah and Matthew's parents were so happy. They each took turns counting not ten, but twenty little toes and twenty little fingers. Angelle and Anjo were really in awe at this new day.

Papa God often referred to this as a labor of love. Angelle and Anjo now understood what He meant. This Miracle of Life was truly a labor of love for this new family.

Angelle and Anjo would be with Sarah and Matthew all their days on Earth. What a wonderful world this will be, they thought. Yes! What a wonderful world full of adventures for the four of them.

Many more adventures to come!

BABY GROWTH FACTS

BEFORE CREATION - God names all His children before He creates them.

DAY 1 - life created by God is called conception; known as Creation Day in Heaven; guardian angels are now on duty; the names of God's children to be born are entered in the Big Book in Heaven.

WEEK 1 - the small clumps of cells multiply and attach to the wall of the uterus (the big room); the uterus is also known as the mother's womb.

DAY 22 - the heart is beating; the body is one inch in length.

WEEK 6 - the mother usually finds out that she's pregnant; the baby's brain is now working.

WEEK 8 - the baby sucks its thumb and kicks/swims in the uterus; the body is about two inches in length.

WEEK 10 - the bodies are completely formed down to the fingers and the toes; the baby even has its own fingerprint.

WEEK 12 - all the baby's tiny organs are working (brain, heart, lungs and kidneys); the baby moves around freely in the uterus; the body is about three inches in length.

WEEK 28 - the top and bottom eyelids open, and the baby can now blink.

WEEK 13 to 40 - the baby grows in size only.

WEEK 40 - the baby is born; Heaven celebrates the baby's earthly birthday.

The growth and development facts have been obtained from a variety of medical and other resources. These facts do vary from one resource to the other. G.A.'s on Assignment has been written utilizing these facts.

Let's Talk About . . .

Please note that some of the following things may be challenging for younger children. Select those that would be appropriate.

In this section, children are encouraged to talk with a parent, guardian or teacher.

Children will need a pencil, paper and a ruler for this Let's Talk About... section. At the end, you will have your very own baby chart for the refrigerator.

Children will also need their Bibles. By now each family should have their own children's Bible for treasure hunts—noted by a star(✯).

1   In chapter one, Angelle and Anjo were now on guardian angel duty for God's special twins. Close your eyes and imagine what your very own angel looks like. Draw a picture of your angel, color it and place it on the refrigerator as an angel-reminder for everyone.

2   On page 9, Anjo spotted two tiny clumps of cells floating in a tunnel. It's time to draw what Anjo saw. First, title your page—**Baby Chart**.

    Place a **small dot or period** on the first line of the paper. It's pretty small!

When life begins, the human cells could be smaller than the dot you made. Now, write next to the period: **beginning of life**.

3 On page 14, Sarah's and Matthew's hearts begin to beat in ONLY 22 days and their little bodies are one inch long.

Think about this unbelievable true fact: the heart is recorded beating at 22 days. WOW!

Use the ruler and draw a **one inch line** below the period. Write **22 days old** next to the line and draw a **heart**.

⚡ Treasure Hunting time! God created man in His own image. Find this fact in the:

Old Testament, the Book of Genesis, Chapter 1, Verses 26-27.

⚡ Treasure Hunting time again! Read how God formed man and gave him life in the:

Old Testament, the Book of Genesis, Chapter 2, Verse 7.

⚡ Treasure Hunting—one more time! Now read with a parent the entire story about the creation of the world and mankind. How many days did it take God to create the world? Which day did God rest? Read the:

Old Testament, the Book of Genesis, Chapters 1 and 2.

4   On page 20, Angelle and Anjo have now been on duty for six weeks. They hear the doctor talking on the outside of their living quarters; he is telling the parents that they are expecting.

Write on paper under your last entry: **6 weeks**—mother finds out she's **expecting**.

5   More baby facts for your chart can be found on pages 45 & 46 of Baby Growth Facts:

a) Draw a **two inch line**; write **8 weeks**; write **baby sucks thumb, swims and kicks**;

b) Write **10 weeks**; draw a simple picture of a **little body** to show that the body is formed; draw a **finger** to show that the baby has its own fingerprint. Great Job!

6   Chapters five and six are important chapters. They teach that at twelve weeks, in addition to the little bodies being completely formed, ALL the organs are working!

Draw a **three inch line**; write **12 weeks or 3 months**; write—**ALL organs working**. Write—**most important fact**.

7   Let's have fun! Can you rap? Well, if you can, join Anjo in Chapter Six with his musical composition of Angel Rap. Get your parent to rap with you. This would also be a fun activity for your class.

8   Chapter seven talks of things that a baby does before it is born; find and write them on your paper after your last entry.

9   Chapter eight reveals that babies normally grow in their mother's uterus for 40 weeks. Finish your chart with the following: **13 weeks to 40 weeks—baby grows in size ONLY**!

10 Chapter eight also reveals what God calls the event when the babies are born. **Find God's three words on page 42; make them the last entry on your chart**. Hang your chart on the refrigerator for family to see.

11 When babies are born, their weight is obtained, and they are measured in inches. Ask your mother to share these facts about you.

    a) Cut a piece of ribbon or string your birth length. Compare your length with others.

    b) Experience how much you weighed at birth. Buy your birth weight in jelly beans; place them in a plastic bag for you to hold. When this is done, share your jelly beans with family and friends. Delicious and fun! (Other items may be substituted for candy.)

About the Author

photo credit: Sheryl O'Meara

Arlene Hebert, born in the small town of Jean-erette, Louisiana, was the oldest daughter and the second child of nine children. She attended and graduated from a small Catholic school and left home in 1969 to attend Charity Hospital School of Nursing in New Orleans, Louisiana. Upon graduation in 1972, she moved to Lafayette, Louisiana, where she worked as a registered nurse for a Catholic hospital for twenty-seven plus years. She also graduated in 1987 with a B.S. in Professional Arts from St. Joseph's College in Standish, Maine.

She is married, has two daughters, a son-in-law and one grandson.

Arlene saw herself retiring in the field of nursing, but God had other plans for her. In 1994, as interesting things began to happen to her, she realized the new direction for her life: writing stories for children. Since writing was never a passion of hers, none of this made any sense.

In 1995, the hospital where she worked decided to close the department she managed, and soon after she was asked to begin a medical auditing program. Arlene couldn't help noticing God's hand in all this when she learned she had to write professionally. She attended educational programs to develop those necessary writing skills.

It was during this time that Arlene explored the idea of writing children's stories. She met two women, Shirley Comeaux and Nancy Burns, whom she credits with leading her down the unfamiliar path of writing for children. Today, they are joined by Joyce Michel, and together these three ladies edit her stories. To date, Arlene has six completed manuscripts; five in the Angeltale Adventure Series.

God continues to be the unseen guide in Arlene's writing career. She is slowly learning to trust Him as she sees things coming to pass without her doing.

A friend, Dr. Huey Stevens, said it best to Arlene, "One day, you need to write the real story–the story behind all the stories."

About the Illustrator

photo credit: Allison Bohl

Peter Berchman DeHart grew up in Lafayette, Louisiana. He attended the Savannah College of Art and Design where he received his degree in Industrial Design and graduated as Salutatorian. He currently resides in his home town of Lafayette and works as a freelance designer, illustrator and painter.

He's also a musician and member of the band, Brass Bed, and frequently tours throughout the United States.

Other Angeltale Books

The Angeltale Adventure Series is presently composed of five stories. These angel stories can be read to younger children, while older children will delight in the stories themselves. Written in small chapters, these stories capture the imagination of six to ten year old children. While the stories are fiction, they teach many different life lessons in an accepting way.

In **Angels in Training: Twin Angel School**, God's plan to create a unique set of twins with special gifts had all of Heaven excited. Most student angels worked hard, hoping to be the chosen team for the assignment. By the end of the story, the reader learns who God selected for this important mission and why. The story portrays God as a loving Father and Teacher who is patient and kind, with a great sense of humor.

In **Angels in Training: Advanced Studies**, God is involved in the education of His chosen team of guardian angels, Angelle and Anjo. He escorts them to two important centers in Heaven, the Angelization Center and the Inspiration and Message Center, where two archangels carry out God's wishes. When formal training is over, God has other surprises for Angelle and Anjo. More adventures are on the horizon!

In **Angels in Training: Promised Adventures**, Anjo flies with Archangel Michael to the Warring

Angel Headquarters, the Kingdom of Lost Souls, and Earth where he witnesses evil at work. Through his adventures, Anjo learns how guardian angels and warring angels work together as Angel-Brothers.

Angelle accompanies Celeste, the Angel of Love and Beauty, to the Valley of Peace, a respite center for God's angels. Here she learns about dreams and how God uses them, about true beauty and why contrast in the world is so important.

When their time with Celeste and Michael is over, they return to Twin Angel School for graduation with the other student angels. The story ends with the long-anticipated event, the creation of the twins. The adventures on Earth are about to begin!

In **G.A.'s on Assignment**, Angelle and Anjo are transported to Earth and arrive in the uterus of the mother-to-be. There they witness first-hand the development of two single cells into Sarah and Matthew. Angelle's and Anjo's adventures continue in their new home for the next forty weeks and end with the births of the twins. Actual growth and development facts are woven into the story and teach children about life in a very creative and accepting way. This story promises to make its readers smile, giggle and laugh.

In **The Chosen Four,** angels are summoned to the Mission Center in Heaven where everything on Earth is monitored, including sports. The angels are briefed on God's plan to change how sports are to be played; and Angelle, Anjo and the twins are part of it. The plan is transmitted to Angelle and Anjo on Earth. They can't wait to share the exciting news with their assignments. Adventures await the four of them in Heaven! This story teaches children about participating in sports for different reasons other than winning. It also focuses on the importance of being together and having fun.